For Sam

First published in paperback in Great Britain
by HarperCollins Children's Books in 2008

ISBN-13: 978-0-00-725866-6
ISBN-10: 0-00-725866-6

1 3 5 7 9 10 8 6 4 2

HarperCollins Children's Books is a division of HarperCollins Publishers Ltd.

Text and illustrations copyright © Emma Chichester Clark 2008
The author/illustrator asserts the moral right to be identified as the author/illustrator of the work.
A CIP catalogue record for this title is available from the British Library.

Visit our website at: www.harpercollinschildrensbooks.co.uk

Printed in Hong Kong

Melrose and Croc

A HERO'S BIRTHDAY

by Emma Chichester Clark

HarperCollins *Children's Books*

In the early morning, as the sun rose,

two friends arrived at a villa, by the sea.

"This is going to be your best birthday ever!"

Melrose said to Croc.

Croc looked around. "It's wonderful!
You are such a kind friend."
"Just don't look in any of the boxes!" said
Melrose. "I'll be back soon."

"But where are you
going?" cried Croc.
"Surprise!" said Melrose.
"But I don't need
any more surprises!"
said Croc.
"This is a surprise
you will really love!"
smiled Melrose.

Down in the harbour, Melrose asked Pierre if
he could borrow his boat for a little while.
"Of course," Pierre said, "but there's a storm
coming, so don't be long."

As Melrose rowed out to sea, he imagined the look on Croc's face when he gave him a fish for breakfast!

He would be over the moon! But Melrose hadn't
noticed how black the sea was, or how dark the
sky had become.

While Melrose
was gone, Croc
explored the garden.
He picked a lovely
bunch of flowers
for the table and got
everything ready.

Then he waited for Melrose. It seemed like ages.

Had something happened to him?

Suddenly Croc felt alone and afraid.

"I'll go and look for him," he thought.

But it was horrible outside – rain was pouring down as Croc ran towards town. There was no one to ask, until he met Pierre, who shouted, "Zat crazy dog 'e's in my boat! I told him – *ze storm is coming!*"

"Oh no!" gasped Croc.

Croc ran at top speed
to the town binoculars.
Desperately he scanned
the stormy sea.

"Where are you?" he
cried to the wind.
"Where are you?"

And then, all his worst
fears came true as he
saw a tiny boat with
a yellow dog inside it.

Croc ran to the lifeboat station.

"Help! Help!" he cried. "You've got to save my friend!

Please help me save my friend!"

The alarm bell rang and all the men ran to the lifeboat.

Huge waves crashed on to the deck, shocking and cold, but Croc didn't notice. Suddenly he saw the little green boat.

"*There he is!*" he shouted. "Can we save him?"

"We'll do everything we can," said the lifeboat man.

"I hope he can hold on."

"Melrose!" cried Little Green Croc. "Hold on, *please, hold on!* We're coming!"

As the lifeboat came closer, a giant wave smashed into Melrose's boat and threw him out, into the sea.

Before anyone could stop him, Croc dived over the side of the lifeboat.

He held on tightly to
Melrose and swam
through the waves.
Then the lifeboat
men pulled them up.

"Well done, little Croc!"
they said.
"You saved my life!"
gasped Melrose.

"I was so scared!" said Croc.

"But you were so brave!" said Melrose.

"I thought I'd lost you," said Croc, and a tear slid down his cheek.

"I wanted to catch a fish for you," said Melrose,
"and now I've ruined your birthday."
"Actually," sniffed Croc, "so far, it's the most
exciting birthday I've ever had!"

As they came into the harbour, there were crowds of people, cheering. Croc's eyes filled with tears again.

"Am I really a hero?" he asked.

"A real hero," said Melrose. "And a true friend."

They were presented with flowers and a beautiful fresh fish.

"Let's go home and open your presents!" said Melrose.

"But I'm so happy," said Croc, "I don't need any presents, I have you, *and* a fish!"

That evening, as the sun went down, Melrose and Croc
sat down to tea.

"Thank you for being there, Croc," said Melrose.

"What would I do without you?"

"I don't know!" said Croc. "What would I do

without... *let's make a wish!*"

"I wish…" whispered Melrose.

"I wish…" whispered Croc.

But neither of them heard what the other had

said, as the sky suddenly exploded with fireworks.

"Happy birthday, dear Croc!" said Melrose.